Ghosted

A NOVELETTE

RUMER HAVEN

fallen·monkey

Also by Rumer Haven

Myths, Mothers, and Mystics
Coattails and Cocktails
What the Clocks Know
Seven for a Secret

Fallen Monkey Press

"Ghosted" first published in *Ghosts & Gravity* by Locklear Books, 2022
Published by Fallen Monkey Press, August 2024

ISBN: 978-1-9998197-7-4

10 9 8 7 6 5 4 3 2 1

Cover Design by RoseWolf Design
Interior Book Design by Coreen Montagna

Printed in the United States of America

To Love.

Preface

Well, look who's *finally* publishing a new story…except it isn't new. And it's already been published.

Lemme explain.

I wrote this story in 2021 for an anthology that would be released the following year. A limited anthology for charity, *Ghosts & Gravity* (Locklear Books, 2022) supported VETSports, a non-profit organization that provides veterans with opportunities to reintegrate into their communities through sports, community service, events, and partnerships. Yet, as "limited anthology" would imply, this compilation wasn't meant to last forever.

So, having reclaimed the rights to my story contribution, I'm bringing it into the fold of Fallen Monkey Press, where it may climb up another tree and screech back out into the world — just in time to celebrate the ten-year anniversary of my first published novel, *Seven for a Secret* (Omnific Publishing, 2014), another work of historical fiction set in a haunted apartment. Both stories also involve the love and loss of single twenty-somethings, but whereas *Seven for a Secret* alternates between 1920s and Y2K Chicago, *Ghosted* takes place in 1970s New York.

Now a standalone novelette, *Ghosted* is indeed its own story. It was always meant to be. That being said, as part of the original anthology project, we authors were required to set our stories in the same Manhattan apartment building (The Wellraven) and in the same year (1972). We were also encouraged to collaborate with each other if we saw any crossover potential between our stories. Weaving these common threads through the anthology really brought The Wellraven to life as a three-dimensional community of tenants (and ghosts and demons, as it were), and while I could easily strip out the crossovers that appear in my story so it can truly stand on its own, I wouldn't dare isolate Apt. 801 like that. It is, and always will be, a prime bit of real estate to be found within The Wellraven, not just a part of its blueprint but its very fabric.

To honor this creative collaboration, then, I'd like to recognize the other authors whose stories and characters have added texture to mine. The redhead next door, for instance, in Apt. 802 is Lucinda from "The Guardian," by Shani Struthers. The, er, rather rambunctious couple upstairs is from Becca Vry's "Chrysalide" and includes Amy, who styles my protagonist Keith's hair. The older couple and child living across the hall are from Morgan and Jennifer Locklear's "Robert," and the shy brunette whom Keith occasionally encounters in the stairwell is Elizabeth from Susan Swords's "Harry Nilsson Was Right." As for more *otherworldly* encounters, the man Keith sometimes sees in his sleep — the one who asks for Sophie — is from "The Man in White" by Ai Tran. And the seductive siren glowing within the walls is none other than the titular demon of D.L. Hartman's debut, "BellaLoki." Many thanks to the above for sharing their time and creativity and if they gave Keith some apartment space in their stories, too. That dear boy needs all the love he can get.

And I, for one, do love him dearly. I set out to write a ghost story and wrote a love story instead (though don't worry, there are definitely still ghosties). But even more than this is a tale of romantic love, it's about *self*-love and accepting yourself even when others don't. So, love and be loved, dear readers, just don't forget to love you, too. ❤

Rumer Haven

July 2024

Ghosted

September 1972

"We never use this room. Why don't we ever use this room?"
No need.

"But this room is nice. Like, *really* nice. And look at the size of it! Bigger than the whole rest of the place." And fully furnished.

No use.

"No, we don't use this furniture either, do we. Why don't we?"
Why you…oh, why, why, why…

"Y'mean, why don't *I*? I don't know…"

Looking around in the dim light that casts large, angular shadows along the inky blue walls of night, Keith squints at all the pale-sheeted ghosts staring back at him. He reaches out at the one nearest him, the one coming up only to his thigh, and grasps the dusty white cotton cover, gently drawing it off the squat form like he's undressing a lover.

"Stereo, too. A really fine one. Top-of-the-line one. Why don't we use this?" Running a hand along the wooden console and lifting its lid to the turntable, it feels fuzzy to the touch, soft and…wrong somehow. Disoriented, slowed, like moving through water, he looks back at the door he's just stepped through, the door he'd never noticed was there before, just off the dining area. On the wall he always thought was just a wall between his apartment and his neighbor's. "Wild, man…right?"

Too late.

Keith steps up to the door and absently lays his hand on the knob. "It's cool in here. I'm actually cold." Then words register, and, twisting back around, Keith pinches his brow at his shadowy companion, who's growing fainter within the ever-darkening room. "But it's not too late. Is it?"

The figure turns its palms up, saying nothing before the cool brass slips from Keith's grasp —

And with a slam, Keith wakes up.

Opening his eyes to the navy of nighttime — that part's the same — he feels the heat before he sees he's back in his bedroom. That part's not the same. And it's not actually his room but the spare one. Not his, really, but *now* his. And now *only* his, not theirs. Not like the other one, the only one they'd needed. All *he'd* needed and ever wanted.

The cold he felt is now barely tepid, whatever relief to be eked from the electric fan's blow meeting the moisture of his slick skin and sweat-soaked sheets…sheets…not ones from the room…the room he forgot…the room he'd never known about in the first place…the one he's already forgetting now…

Squeezing his eyes shut, Keith breathes in the thick, humid air and exhales out all the hope he'd felt in the discovery so that the pain can retake its place.

The room isn't there. Never was.

And neither was Roderick.

Slam!

Seizing his breath, Keith is startled awake to a now yellow room, baking in the sunshine beaming through bare windows.

He's twisted in his bedsheet, binding him tighter to this place, refusing to let him go. No. No, that's not the case. Can't be when he doesn't want to be let go. Doesn't, himself, want to let go.

Loosening the corner of perspiration-dampened cloth from its stranglehold around his neck, Keith brings it to his face, breathes it in deeply, and then chokes his sobs into it when the scent carries nothing of Rod, who'd felt so real…

Gasping out a last whimper, Keith wipes his eyes on a mustard-yellow dandelion printed on the cotton sheet. Finally, he sits up, wills himself to detangle from the bed and stand up. Takes a step away from it. Then two. One step at a time. That's all it takes, all he can manage. At this lethargic pace, he drags one foot then the other through discarded denim and terry cloth, out the door and into the living room. Grinding his gaze to his left, he stares at the rear dining room wall. No door. As he thought. Just that actress's place next door. What is that crazy redhead's deal anyway? The thumps and thuds that come from there around the clock are weird to no end, and don't even get him started on the couple upstairs.

With his gaze fixed on that patch of avocado-green wall where he'd sworn only hours ago there'd been a door to a whole other, unused section of furnished apartment space, Keith walks to the dining room table and slumps down on one of its uncomfortable vinyl-and-chrome chairs. Air hisses from the seat pad under his weight, and he deflates along with it, resting his elbow on the wood-grain Formica table surface and his sluggish head on his knuckles. Lazily, he thumbs through yesterday's unread newspaper with his other hand, willing to connect this much with the outside world as he casts a glance at the beige telephone on the kitchen countertop that never rings anymore. Sighing with mixed relief and regret, he flips to the sports section.

"The Munich Games: Readers' Reactions to Controversies Surrounding Games," reads page seven of the *New York Times*. In the days to follow the massacre—when the Games themselves have already ended—that people would still write in to complain about Olympic judging and "spirit"… *Honestly*, Keith thinks.

Eleven athletes died, were killed, executed, but apparently readers still want to know why a player would be disqualified for asthma medication or why coaches called time-out when they did. What horseshit, Rod would say. Probably does say, wherever he is.

Keith slaps the paper closed in disgust, sick with how dark and diseased 1972 has become before summer's even met its end. Could there be a more blackened year…kicked off with Bloody Sunday in Northern Ireland, the Troubles escalating ever since, then this recent terrorism in Munich, piled on by Watergate, Vietnam…and lest he forget Roderick, as if he ever could…

So many times and for so many reasons, Keith has wished one night he'll fall asleep and wake up in some far-off year like 2020, where the future will have everything figured the fuck out and won't know nightmares like this. *It'll* have *to be better than this…won't it?*

Sighing, he closes his eyelids and rubs them vigorously with his middle finger and thumb. Then he heaves a deep yawn and looks up, sucks his tongue against the roof of his mouth in a desperate attempt at moisture as he glances past the counter of the adjoining kitchen to the master bedroom doorway just beyond. The door is closed, as it always is. Sealing off the tomb of what was but would never be again. He knows it won't be, that it can't be. Somehow, he *knows*.

There was a time when he'd held out faith Rod would come back, that he'd express his remorse and beg Keith for forgiveness, and of course Keith would take him back—maybe not immediately, maybe not until he'd made him sweat it out a little and truly show he was sorry and sincere about that second chance… after which he'd *really* make him sweat it out, in the better way that they both would enjoy, but now…

Now he knows there'll be no second chance. He knows it in the marrow of his bones.

He just doesn't know why.

"I don't understand. Why don't we ever use this room?"

His shadow companion shrugs, gives a deep, dark chuckle, slow and thick like honey. Keith thinks it's Rod again, but he can't be sure. He's pretty sure, though. Yeah. It's him. Gotta be.

"But we're here all the time. Complaining this place's too small. Why don't we ever use this part of it? Why don't we ever open this door?"

At this, the other being—who is or isn't Rod but feels like it could be—seems to sober. His—its—expression can't be made out, though. Not as clearly as before. The face is…less. Not quite a face. Yet a blackened hole grows where a face would be and says, *Not all doors…meant to open.*

Pulling the sheet off a console television, Keith snorts. "What? 'Course they are. That's what they're *for*. If we weren't meant to open them, why have doors?"

Yes, open…

"Yeah? But?"

Not until…

"They're meant to be."

A silent nod.

"And we weren't."

Rod's—its—image goes jagged a second, does so again every now and then, like when a TV antenna needs adjusting. *Weren't…what?*

"Opened. We couldn't open."

Aren't doors.

"Aren't meant to be either."

Doors?

"To be."

Why?

"You know why."

You.

"Oh, so it's *my* fault?"

Why?

"That's what I'd like to know."

Oh, why, why, why?

On a sharp inhale, Keith wakes and sits up. It's still dark out. Streetlamps project disorienting trapezoids onto the walls, like forced perspective, cerulean cutouts in the deeper midnight blue. He is topless and sweating, and, panting, he clasps the gold pendant hanging from his neck, scraping it from where it's adhered to his sticky skin.

"Rod?" he asks, though the name sounds caught in the humid air, muffled, until he realizes it didn't even escape his throat. It's his mind that screams it clearly, more crisply than it could come to him in the dream, resolved to a finer precision than he could even see the face, than he could even see if there *was* a face. If there'd ever been. He couldn't know it was him, didn't know at all, and he never even touched him, yet still he felt him, could *smell* him. He sensed him in every other possible way, ways unknown to himself, ways he can't remember now, for whatever was lost to his sight.

"Roderick," he says sternly, though it's carried on a sob. He releases the necklace to hold his face in his hands, his eyes streaming into already dampened palms that he now breathes in deeply, feverishly, trying to detect any last, lingering scent of his love, his heart. Gone. Vanished, like he did in real life.

A knot in Keith's chest twists as the memory wrings the last of his fortitude from him. Only two months have passed since he last looked into those brown eyes, looked lovingly, imploringly at that strong brow that seemed to pinch in spite of Rod's self, the self that was leaving, walking away, and not just that but into the arms of someone else. Where had it gone so wrong? Keith knew what it looked like, the words that were said, but his heart saw and heard so much more than that; he knew it did, communicating on a vibration matching Rod's that didn't require anything to be said, that didn't need to look like anything other than what it was, because that was all just optics, just for everyone else. All that mattered was the two of them and what they knew between each other, even if one of them didn't know it yet.

Would Rod ever know? Will he come back? Heaving forward under the weight of his leaden, emptying lungs, Keith grasps at the chain sticking to his chest and, this time, yanks it off.

Glinting in the light of a new day, which narrowly escapes through the heavy brown-gold dupioni drapes, the delicate, severed ends of Keith's necklace won't grow back together at his thumb's touch. He twiddles with the chain, weaving it between his fingers, and feels sick over the broken link that won't bring everything full circle again.

The jewelry was a gift. Not for Keith but *from* him. For Rod, who owned a dozen necklaces and rings and things far finer than that, but Keith had wanted to make his mark on him somehow, tag him, possess him, which he knew even at the time was wrong. That isn't something to do to someone — ever — let alone someone you love, but it's how desperate that man would make him feel, like Rod was forever slipping through his fingers as this thread of gold does now. There was no predicting him, committing him, and all Keith wanted was some kind of anchor to keep them tethered together. That was a possessive love, an *ob*sessive one, he knew it, he *knows* that, but it was his first one, the one he hadn't known how badly he needed until Rod had shown him the way, shown him who he really is and made him want to be possessed, too. Taken and submissive.

Sliding his gaze toward the bare dining-area wall, Keith sees another door that hadn't opened for him until it did. Another threshold he hadn't crossed until he did, with Rod, and felt the white-hot light kiss his face, illuminate everything trying to slither out of view, hiding in shadow. He'd been naked and exposed, at last, and Rod was his sun god, heating the dormant waters of a deep well within him until they steamed to the surface and he exploded.

Still fondling the chain, Keith watches its coin pendant slip to the floor. He stares at it pensively for a moment before stretching down to snag it out from the crusted shag carpet. Pinching the disk, he brings it between his teeth and bites down.

Another evening, but this time Keith can't sleep, can't escape into that recess behind the dining room wall. He sits instead in the adjacent living area, slumped down on his lumpy couch while he zones out at his television set, the screen gone to static.

The heat has passed its peak, but the backs of his legs still sweat into the polyester velour that smothers him from behind, flooding the farm scene printed in rusts, greens, and browns on the cream-colored cushion. He adjusts the crotch of his tight jean shorts, and the corresponding movement of his slender hips allows a cooling pillow of air to sneak beneath his sinewy thighs, offering more relief.

Losing his sight into the snowy screen of the cathode-ray tube, Keith almost feels its frost, wants to warm it with an image, but what? He liked an army program that premiered recently — based on that movie, the one about doctors in the Korean War, pretty funny. But more than it made him laugh, it reminded him of the dog tags Roderick would wear in protest of today's war, his personal "medals of honor." He's old enough to avoid the draft, but Keith isn't, only able to dodge because, as a Quaker, he can conscientiously object. He could get a pass on another technicality, of course, had his evangelical roots not sealed his lips on that. There was so much Rod could've loved Keith for, did love him for, but for that — his conditioned shame or, at best, shyness over his truth — for that, Rod would always loathe him. That much was plain.

"If you can't be honest with yourself," Rod would say, *"how'm I supposed to trust you're honest with me? That you're not ashamed of me also?"* Keith knew he meant it, too, every goddamn time he said it, and yet the dramatic lilt of his voice tended to give away what an awfully convenient excuse it also was to keep Keith at

arm's length. To push him away—until yanking him back so closely they'd fuse together in seconds. Merge into one. Just to smash apart again, broken bits of himself lost in the process each time. Now Keith can't put himself back together any more than he can that necklace.

The snowy television crackles, then zaps.

M*A*S*H. That was the show. The first night it aired was also the first night he dreamed about Rod, finding him in that nonexistent "room" when Keith couldn't find him anywhere else in his waking life. At least, he thinks it was Rod—the past nights, too—but the only really vivid things in the visions are those furnishings in that room. That damned room. *He'll* be damned if he ever goes back in there. He won't.

Eyelids now heavy in the heat, he sinks farther down on his sofa and eventually kicks his legs up onto it, swiveling to recline along its length despite the plush print baking into his body and his denim shorts digging into his dick again. To the crackle of the television, he drifts off to silly thoughts…imagining the sofa's ugly old barns seeping from its fabric into his skin, then him actually slipping down into one, falling yet landing softly and waking in a fully furnished horse stall, its hay bales covered in sheets; it's got a TV and stereo in there, too, and coming from somewhere up in the loft is a series of repetitive clicks, like a rotary phone dialing—

Slam!

Keith jolts up from where he's dozed on the sofa. Dizzily, he sets one foot then the other on the shag carpet, trading one fuzzy sensation for another as he finally abandons the tacky barnyard of his Colonial Revival couch—the one Rod used to give him such tremendous shit for—to stride toward where he thinks the sound came from. The sound he's heard before, like a door slamming, but…in the dining room? He walks to the table, dings a knee on a chair as he steps around it to stand face-to-face with the wall. He presses his hand on a seam of its textured wallpaper. Tapping the pads of his fingers against the unyielding hardness, he snorts out an exhale and drops his head, snickering in mockery at what a dunce he must be to think for a second there could be a door there. Again, all that's on the other side is Lucinda's apartment.

With his one palm still pressed on the wall, he runs the other through his hair, easing the fine, honey-brown strands out of his eyes and then wiping his hand down his face, stopping it at the uncharacteristic stubble that's grown at his jaw. What his hairdresser would think if she saw him now—not at the salon, obviously, where she'd buffed him as shiny as an Emmy for that audition he never made it to—but in the halls and elevators of The Wellraven itself, where she and her husband live just upstairs.

If Keith were to venture outside of 801 again, that is. It's been weeks since he has, not since his last attempt to find Rod at one of their old haunts, where the fellas seemed only too happy to inform Keith about Rod's northern migration with Ty, another client he represents. An even younger model of Keith; they only ever seem to get younger the more Rod advances into his forties, refusing to age. That was August, though Keith had already heard the first whisperings of the affair back in July, the day he'd gotten the casting call and swiftly booked his appointment with Amy at Upper East Dyed. Then the night before the audition, he got to see it for himself—got to see a lot more of Ty, with Rod, beneath a neon light, than he'd ever wanted to. Not even trying to hide it.

The next day, when Keith ended up auditioning for leading man of a corner barstool instead of the supporting TV role, there was no angry call from his agent afterward. No contact whatsoever. No agent. No Rod. Not anymore. As he would learn soon enough.

No, Amy wouldn't be thrilled with how he's let her creation go since that summer of his discontent. Whose sweet, baby-faced boy does he need to be anymore anyway, now that the jobs have dried up right along with his agent's representation. Rod once told him that it paid to be pretty, that he'd see to it Keith got paid pretty damn well for it, too, if Keith trusted Rod to groom him, schmooze him, put him in front of any bite he could get before putting him in front of himself to take his own nibbles of that golden flesh. The seduction was simple; Rod tried harder than he ever needed to, but how Keith liked to watch him try. Back when he did. Knowing he was trying—and succeeding—with so many others, too, like the one he's with now. All the pretty boys.

Curling his fingers into a claw, Keith digs his nails into the heat-softened wallpaper and scrapes them down the swirling textured surface, managing to tear it in one spot. Sadly, he looks to the jagged rip, pinches at the crinkled strip he's peeled away and, licking his thumb for some saliva sealant, tries to smooth it back into place. Just like he thought he could meld the ends of his necklace chain back together, always kidding himself that he can heal, that separation is only temporary and that things can come back together if only he wills it enough.

What a weak will he has, though; what a weak man he is. He can't repair what's so broken and doesn't understand why he even tries.

Gliding the pad of his thumb over the wrinkled scrap of paper, he then pinches the shred to yank it off, slicing a deeper wound into the wall.

Go ahead and bleed, he says. *See if I care.*

Then he walks to the second bedroom and closes the door behind him on what dreaded dreams might come.

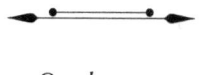

October 1972

Days, dreams, and drinks multiply until, one night, blood does seep down the wall from where Keith peeled the paper away. The spot right next to the door, which this time doesn't open. Won't. He slams against it, kicks at it, punches his fist through it, but whatever cracks and holes he splits and punctures, they seal right back up, like they were never there.

"*You're* never here either! You're not!" Keith unleashes his fury and spit at the dark and deceiving door. "You're not real!

This isn't…" Slapping his palm on the coarse wooden surface, he catches his breath and sinks to his knees. Turns his back on the wall and slumps against it. "This isn't real."

Rod is behind that door; Keith knows it, but he's not letting him in. Not this time, and Keith wants to blame him but doesn't, because none of this is real. Rod isn't real, not anymore, not in Keith's life, anyway. Just a figment, a memory that made its mark then left it behind. A scar on Keith's heart, now on the wall, but the man doesn't exist. He's gone.

Just when Keith starts to accept that, at least for now so he can sleep, he senses his spine sinking into a rubbery surface behind him, now gelatinous…and cold, so very cold, and it tingles over him like slippery static until he's fallen back into the room.

He lies on his back now at the room's center, between the sheet-covered armchairs and sofa, and he stares up at an illuminated chandelier, the crystals shimmering and trembling overhead like frightened diamonds, wishing he hadn't come. They vibrate and shiver as if shaking their heads at him, mourning the mistake, the misplacement of someone like him here, and then a shadow dims their suffering, crawls across their sparkling light like a widow's veil to dull Keith's view.

Not all doors…meant to open.

It's getting colder, so much colder while a touch — as if made of a million grains of sand yet not solid — begins to caress over his arm, his wrist. Then it glides over both arms, moves through his hands and up, encircling his fine wrist bones and pulsing in sync with the beat of his heart.

Keith's chest sinks as he feels a pressure bear down on him, not heavy but perceptible, a presence elongating over his form and moving ever closer, closer…and then static sparks his lips, and with a gust of air on his face —

It's gone. His chest reinflates with the pressure lifted from it, with only the gold pendant resting on it, slipping a little to the side until its chain hooks on one of his shirt buttons. His wrists still tingle, but the veil's been drawn away, except he doesn't see the twinkling light fixture overhead. He doesn't see…anything.

And then he opens his eyes.

Feels the sting on his wrists, which are sticking to his bedsheet.

"Shit," he whispers as he wads the fabric tight around his left arm. He rolls to his side, curls up in a ball and cries it out. And then he gets himself to his feet, navigates through the dark, a toe hooking onto something stringlike as he steps from the shag onto the cold tile of the room that will save him...after the other one already did.

His foot skids a little on the floor, grinding something against the laminate, and on flicking the light on, he sees he's dragged in the broken necklace chain, its pendant barely hanging on near the lobster clasp. Reaching for it, he wraps it in a faded pear-green face cloth and stuffs it in a vanity drawer. Then he inspects the damage: his right arm has just a scratch, a burn, more like, where he kept rubbing it against the tear in the wallpaper as if he could smudge it out, fervently scrubbing and scrubbing until red-hot pain seared through his wrist, and Keith liked that he felt something. For a second, he blindingly forgot about Roderick and his own pathetic demise and thought nothing but felt, fell into the pain and wanted more.

No one came knocking when he smashed a whiskey bottle against the kitchen floor, the last inch of its honey-colored contents creeping across the harvest-gold linoleum and blotting out its floral pattern like Keith had tried to blot his memory with the booze. No such luck, and he was determined that he wouldn't dream tonight, wouldn't dream ever again once a shard's sweet kiss to his wrist sent him to sleep for good.

Except it didn't work. Or maybe it would have, if he hadn't entered that room...*the* room, the one just beyond, here yet not here, which is how Keith has been feeling, too, trying to find his place. Fuck if it's The Wellraven. He really should go. Leave this place and what seeps into and stays in its walls. Leave this city altogether and what stains its streets...*Ciao, Manhattan.*

Nothing he can do about it now, though. Standing over the cornflower-blue sink in the guest bathroom, one of the bulbs flickers then snuffs out behind the trough fixture overhead. Other bulbs remain lit behind the frosted, gold-filigreed white glass, but the new dimness casts a pallid, cadaverous light onto Keith's face, his jade eyes almost brown, and he imagines for a moment that he can see through himself in the mirror, that either he's translucent or what he's seeing is actually *behind* the glass, a window to the other room that's there but not there. Teetering on his bare feet, he zones out at his reflection for a moment, sees the glass begin to ripple like water around it until—

A deep breath and a blink later, it's gone. Whatever it was. The mirror is solid, as Keith confirms with a tap of his fingertip, and he himself looks solid, the only room he can see in the glass now just the one behind him. Shaking his head, he bends over the sink and runs some tepid water over his wrist to clean out the wound that isn't as deep as he thought.

As autumn leaves fade and fall, Keith's body heals if his heart doesn't. After that scare, those depths he hadn't known he could drop into, he's actually made some effort to get out of this stuffy place, mingle with some humanity again, though the bustle outside always drives him back in before too long.

Coming and going from The Wellraven, he sticks to the stairs, not keen on elevator small talk, and he'd hate for the old folks and sickly little kid across the hall to see him like this; they always look like they've got enough on their minds, and he wouldn't want to add to their worries that their neighbor's a psycho. Lucinda, too, the lively redhead next door, would only want to talk shop, swap headshots...question why he doesn't audition or have an agent or come to her parties anymore. So, in the refuge of the stairwell, all he's ever encountered is a young brunette, who only goes as far as the second floor. She seems as shy and keen to keep to herself as Keith, so no bother there.

He's supposed to be looking for a new place, and probably a job, but his feet only ever lead him to Central Park, just six blocks west. Roderick always wanted to go there together, but Keith didn't, not with Rod, not in the daytime; he liked their life in the dark, in private—or "hidden," as Rod would bitterly accuse. Keith feels cloaked in the dark no matter where he goes, really, but at least the park's one place he can go without a ghost.

Or so he thought. Out of the corner of his eye, he keeps thinking he sees Rod everywhere on the pathways, in the grass, loses his breath at the thought that maybe he's come back, maybe he never left town to begin with. Maybe he'll make his way back to Keith after all. But he would've done that by now.

Maybe. Maybe not. It's the possibility that he could that's the only thing keeping Keith breathing right now. He needs to see Roderick again. He will, and when he does, if Rod can look him in the eye and honestly say he doesn't still love him, well then…then maybe Keith'll just have to finish the job he started that dark, desperate night, and no one in the Room will be able to save him this time.

Keith believed he was over thoughts like this, that he might've turned a corner even if there's still the long road ahead. But this morning when he was fishing around in a bathroom drawer for his razor, thinking it might be time to show his face again, he pulled out a wash rag, and the gold chain fell to the floor, its coin pendant spinning a few inches away. A rush of feeling overcame him, sensations he's mostly, *almost* been spared since hiding the necklace from sight. He immediately abandoned the search for his razor, picking the jewelry up and trying once more to fix it—

And has ended up burying it instead. In Central Park. Clear on the other side, near the exit to West 72nd Street. He feels somewhat better, lighter for it, yet has swung by the liquor store to pick up a little sack "lunch" for himself on his way back to The Wellraven all the same.

He only wants some rest today. Peace. Oblivion. A dreamless sleep where he doesn't have to visit the Room—which he still does every now and then, but the figure he used to think was Rod isn't there anymore. Abandoning Keith even in dreams. Nowadays, Keith usually finds himself alone in the Room, though sometimes there's another guy, dressed all in white, who keeps asking for Sophie, whoever that is, and then last night…

Last night, after Keith fell asleep in front of the TV, he dreamt that a bright light woke him, beaming through the cracks around the nonexistent dining room door. In a haze, he stood and approached the avocado wall, opened the door without questioning, and was nearly blinded by the glow, so piercing it practically hummed in his ears, and he could hardly stand to look if it hadn't already resolved itself into the voluptuous shape of a woman, who extended an arm in invitation. Without speaking, he knew what she wanted, that she enjoys it often and within the very walls of The Wellraven, and Keith couldn't deny he wanted it, too. Needed the sensuous sweetness rolling off of her in waves…

But not in the Room, not where he waits for Rod to come back, even if it could make him jealous.

Instead, Keith backed away from the light and closed the door on it, returning to the couch, where he jacked himself off and finally did sink into the blank of a sleep without dreams. Waking this morning to find his hand sticking to his crusted stomach, he had to question whether the woman had been just a dream after all, but of course, a look at the solid dining room wall reminded him that she must've been and he managed to pleasure himself to the fantasy unconsciously. Yet it felt so real… and even now, he wonders if the luminous woman will ever come back, guide him by the hand to the interior of a different wall, any other wall but that one.

It's not like he hasn't slept with chicks before — and for no better reason than to take the edge off or pass the time. He exclusively did, actually, until his awakening with Rod. And he does find pleasure in them, the softness of their skin and the pillowy swell of their breasts, liberated from cheesecloth and crochet.

Keith typically had his pick of the ladies at clubs, too, a golden god himself back when he was kind of becoming a big deal, a model-turned-actor making the jump from spearmint gum and toothpaste commercials to bit parts in daytime soap operas, thanks to Rod. Also thanks to his agent, he was asked to audition for a recurring role in the relatively new and low-ranking — but promising—*All My Children* back in July. He thought he had it made when that call came in—one of the last rings to jar his kitchen phone—'til Rod never returned to The Wellhaven, so Keith never returned to Pine Valley.

And he can't return home either. Won't. Not to parents he wouldn't introduce Rod to even if his lover had ever asked. Rod didn't, of course, at least not in earnest, Keith's sure, believing that when he did ask it was only to test him. Sometimes Rod just liked to pick fights so they could make up afterwards, but when he poked at Keith with this particular stick and Keith bit back…well, Rod didn't understand, didn't even want to waste the effort fighting, would just grab his jacket and Camels and go.

Sometimes Keith could catch up with him, find him smoking outside the lobby doors, but only rarely could he lure him back upstairs when he got in that kind of mood. Rod didn't want to stay in the dark with Keith, but why would Keith take such a chance with someone he knew, just *knew*, wouldn't be there for him when the walls crumbled down? That it was just a matter of time before Rod would do exactly what he did…

So why Keith should mourn like he does, act so blindsided even months later, it's just making less and less sense with each day.

Fuck. Gotta get out of your head, man. Get him outta your heart. Fuck this. Fuck him, and fuck you, too.

Slamming Door 801 behind him, he lingers in the entryway, unsure what to do with himself, but the crinkle of the brown bag in his grip gives him a good idea. Deciding first to just glare at the closed door to the master bedroom for a while, as if *that'll* show Rod, Keith's senses readjust to the indoor scents of stale alcohol and musty carpet and only the faintest trace of tobacco, held in place by dank air that immediately enshrouds him and suppresses his breath.

The weight of this place…*God*. Heavy, so heavy, and flicking on the pendant lamp in the dining room does little to cut the density. Above the table, the yellowed, wicker-caged orb just swings slightly as footsteps thump from the unit above—Amy's place, which over the summer seemed to pick up in action just when Keith's died down, moaning and groaning from people and furniture alike.

With a sharp clunk, Keith plops his purchase on the counter that separates the kitchen from the dining area and then sheds his thin cognac leather jacket, tossing it on the dining room table, where it slips onto a vinyl chair. He sees dark spots at the base of the lamp's glowing globe — the remains of bugs that flew too close to the light and got themselves trapped. Eyeing the lamp with disdain, he frowns and gives it a good shove, leaving it to swing like a pendulum and cast disorienting shadows all around the apartment, like a dismal disco. Swinging, swinging until the light then starts swirling, making its orbit around dust particles that settle to the tabletop from the brittle, scalloped wicker shade.

And then it stops, just…stops. But not hanging downward above the center of the table — the lamp's suspended at an angle, stretching on its chain from the ceiling toward the dining room wall as though it were metal drawn to a magnet. But neither is either, and Keith doesn't know what he's tripping on right now.

Nothing. He's taken nothing today. Left the drugs behind with the girls at the clubs, but at the moment he could do with something to chill the fuck out.

What in Christ's name…

Slowly sidestepping the chair where his jacket lies slumped as if cowering from what's got Keith freaked, too, he wills himself to round the table and approach the lamp from the other side. Extending a hand, he tentatively waves it between the lamp and the wall as though expecting to find strings attached.

Instead, all he feels is a granular texture, like running his hand through sand, except it's ice-cold…nothing like the sun-baked beach, where Keith would comb the sand with his long, narrow fingers…and Rod would kiss the sea-salted sweat from his shoulder and neck…Riis being one park where Keith was less reluctant to let his sun god shine down on him publicly.

Damn it, there he is again, on Keith's mind when he's trying to exorcise him. But now he feels Rod more intensely than ever.

Fluttering his fingers in that space in between, he stares at the lamp pointing like an arrow at that damn wall, at the gash Keith tore in it. He doesn't hear the thumping overhead anymore, no soft electrical buzz from the lamp, and the fridge has stopped humming in the kitchen. No rush and whir or honks of traffic invade from outside either; it's a pure silence Keith has never known, and all he can hear is the ringing in his own ears, intensifying with every second.

As a slow pressure bears down on his chest, he holds his breath for a moment, confirming the stillness, the absolute lack of sound that his last few exhales didn't even make. In this moment, he thinks his heart might have stopped, too, and he feels the chill creep up his arm and kiss up his neck to his cheeks until —

With his gaze, he follows the line of the lamp to the rip in the wallpaper. Drops his arm and steps toward it, picks at it with his nail. Then, as he tries to smooth the paper back over, he feels a lump in it, just below the tear. He presses his thumb to it, then runs the other along it, too. There's something flat but perceptible under there, and though the wallpaper's textured, he would've for sure seen this slight protrusion before, which casts its own sliver of shadow.

Keith scrapes again at the base of the torn slice of paper, pulling it a little farther away from the wall this time. Some fibers remain behind, maintaining allegiance with the hardened glue, but he sees something glinting in the crevice. He digs in with a nail to pick more of the layer away, eventually excavating a thread of gold. Pinching it, he tries to pull it out, but it resists. Trying and trying again, he finally rips the strip down to create a greater slash in the wall, and something small, metallic, falls onto the toe of his boot.

Keith jerks back. Keeps stepping away with his gaze fastened on the gold chain and coin pendant lying on his dining room floor.

Before he can get his bearings and make any sense of how the necklace found its way into the wall after he's just buried it, the lamp swings away, released from whatever held it. Buzzing, humming, and honking returns, and Keith is just barely able to catch his breath again, just watches the light swinging side to side in ever-diminishing arcs as it loses momentum, hypnotized by it until the lamp's rusted chain ceases creaking against the ceiling hook.

The chill is gone, and now he's almost hot inside this thick, stagnant air, though it's cooled down so much outside. With one last wary gaze at the lamp and then at the wall, Keith inches back and bends to pick up the necklace, breathes in and blows out a big breath as he dusts some dirt off of it and shoves it in his back pocket.

He crosses the living room and throws open the bronze draperies and the champagne sheers behind them. Stepping out onto his balcony, he rests heavily on the short side railing that faces 1st Avenue, the rutted iron digging into his forearms as he watches yellow-taxied traffic beyond his goose-bumped flesh.

The cool breeze brushing through his hair now isn't like what he just felt, though. What that frigid patch of air, like quicksand to the touch, *did* feel like was something he'd experienced in a dream…the one that he thought, for a time, had saved his life, though that was bullshit. Keith didn't carry out what he'd drunkenly decided to do, so there was never any danger, just some bloody dandelions that he couldn't wash the stain out of the next morning and a permanent scar on his left wrist. Just as well that his career's over. He's not meant for anyone's gaze anymore, so what should it matter if he loses his looks one wrinkle and wound at a time.

With his hair dulled of its sun-kissed luster, darkening and growing closer toward his neck as his beard thickens around a more filled-out face, he's starting to look more like Rod, actually, and has sometimes thought he's seen him in the mirror—the same one where he once thought he could look into the Room. He's gotten paler, too, inevitable since summer's end and from holing up at home so much, only ever leaving for food and booze or those aimless walks in the park.

He dreams again of that fantasy future life and wonders what 2020 Keith would be doing. If he'd be living in such isolation or reveling in a freer, happier existence. In a world that accepts him for who he is. With people who love him for it, too.

Because he can't help wondering now how it would be any better if Rod had never left. Where were they destined to go anyway? Rod wouldn't commit any more than Keith would come out. If he's honest with himself, he never saw a future for them, only disaster, only exactly what's happened, and yet…in the moment, the *moments* that suspended them in time…no world around them, no light, no dark, just them breathing life into and sucking it out of each other. If he could've preserved them in amber, then maybe…

Keith's head drops forward on a laugh. He continues laughing into his palm as his fingernails pick the crust from the corners of his eyes. *What the fuck*, he thinks as he straightens and turns to face the second sliding door to his master bedroom, relieved the orange linen curtain is drawn over it so he can't see inside that mausoleum. Biting his lip, he eases his fingers into his back jeans pocket to retrieve the necklace, dangles it in front of his face, and follows it side to side with his gaze like he did with the lamp.

You're cursed, he thinks. The necklace is hexed. He was finally starting to do fine — *I was FINE* — and then it showed up and all hell is breaking loose again.

"It's fucking tiki shit, is what this is," he mutters, having watched the three-part *Brady Bunch* Hawaiian holiday recently, where Bobby found an ancient idol on the island and bad luck befell anyone who wore it. Grimacing at what's gotta be his own jinxed jewelry, he flings the necklace over the railing, not even looking to see where it lands.

Heaving a dry sob, he smears the back of his hand under his nose and stares down the door leading back into the living room.

"I don't know, man," he says on an exhale, and, scratching his scalp feverishly and fluffing his mane out with both hands, he strides back inside — determined not to delude himself with any more of this weird shit. To just watch some fucking TV and mentally escape this life, this building, for a time. And tomorrow, look through some fucking classifieds for a roommate because this living-by-himself business is not working out. He doesn't want a roommate, but he needs one. Not just to pull himself from this emotional hole he's screwed himself firmly into but, financially, he's barely scraping by. And he can't go to his parents. He can't. He won't. For as much as he can't be who he really is with them, he can't stomach pretending he's anyone else either. Can't. Won't.

"I can't!"

"You won't."

That's how the conversation often went with Rod, most recently at the June march. Keith stuck to the sidewalk and watched Rod's thick, dark brown waves flow with the current up Christopher Street. Keith walked in parallel but never stepped off the curb to join the event, beelining it back to The Wellraven once the route ended at Central Park. That was one of the last times Rod would see or speak to him again, as if Keith didn't also stand in solidarity with Stonewall, as if…

Whatever, man.

He doesn't know why he makes the excuses he does for himself. And yet of course he does. It's because his mom's not Jeanne Manford, who marched with her son on that Liberation Day, urging other parents to unite in support of their gay children. It's because, though his family's own Quaker community also publicly declared support for bisexuality over the summer, Keith knows his parents' answer to the Ithaca Statement's first question: No. They are *not* open to examining sexuality with understanding, loving or otherwise, thank you very much. Because they are Friends of some but not Friends to all.

Hissing out a breath as he closes his door on the cool air behind him, Keith marches to the counter and grabs the paper bag from it, rolling the top of it down so he can unscrew and chug what's inside. Then he switches on the TV, turning the dial through a few stations until he lands on one that'll do, and drops onto his ugly couch, casting the occasional side-eye at the dining room lamp and wall.

On the sofa, he wakes to a light yet high-pitched squeak. Then another.

Facedown in his drool, he takes a few seconds to flutter his eyes open, bat away the dryness. The apartment's dark except for the blue glow of the TV, but even that's not as bright as it normally is. From the dining room, the creaking continues, rhythmic, like the pulsing weight of sex on bedsprings.

"*Air…*"

Having momentarily closed his eyes again, Keith pops one open now.

"*…must get ooouut…*"

At the breathy voice, Keith stiffens and, still lying on his stomach, tilts his head up from the velvety cushion to look in the direction of the dining area, half expecting to see the glow of the woman in the walls.

"*…must haaave aaair…*"

Propped up on his elbows now, Keith swivels his face toward the sound of moaning coming from the other side of the living room. There, in the muted light of the TV, he sees—

A ghost.

Rising from the opened lid of an old trunk.

Shining…translucent…

And clearly made of cellophane. Yet Bobby and Peter Brady are scared shitless and shouting for Greg to wake up.

Heaving out an exhale, Keith drunkenly giggles to himself, then cackles wildly out loud as he rolls over onto his back at what must be a prank by the Brady sisters. He'd know Marcia's sultry whisper anywhere, having had his share of fantasies involving Maureen McCormick but mostly Barry Williams.

Jesus, that scared him, though. Yet it's nothing near as jolting as the telephone now ringing from the kitchen. Shrill, shrieking, throbbing through his heavy head that he pickled in whiskey, starting early enough in the day that he apparently passed out by prime time.

That fucking phone hasn't rung in weeks, and he sure as shit doesn't want to answer it now. But doesn't want to listen to it anymore either.

So he stands up, swaying with the effort and having to catch himself once with a step back before ambling forward to the sound. Mustering all the concentration his blurry brain can whittle together, he crosses the living room and bumps into a dining room chair. Reaching an arm out and feeling around the side wall, he finds the light switch and turns it on to see the pendant lamp swinging just slightly.

The phone on the counter between the kitchen and dining space continues to rattle through its rings, so Keith reaches for that next only to lift the receiver then slam it back down.

Silence. Except for the creaking of the lamp vacillating on its rusted chain. Keith side-eyes it and wonders if his own inebriated steps or ones upstairs set it in motion this time. At least it's dangling normally, though, no magnetic pull to the back wall like this afternoon, which he decided to drink, rather than explain, away. The way it had angled toward the wall, like it was pointing, right at…wanting him to find it…

Keith looks at the tear in the wallpaper. Steps toward it, picks at it some more with his nail. Loses interest and stumbles back to the sofa to watch *The Partridge Family* and then pass out to *Ghost Story*.

Be one.

"Be one what?"

Bee.

"What?"

See.

"What am I supposed to see?"

One sea.

Exasperated, Keith flails his arms out and he spins, looking at everything in the Room and having no idea what he's being directed to do. It isn't the woman in here with him this time, but he can't be sure it's Rod either. Only a blackened shadow that seems more defined by the negative space around it than any actual form of its own.

"Roderick. If this is you, I don't understand. Where are you? What are you trying to tell me?"

Why?

"*Why?* Why do you think? Because you just up and left, and if this is the only way I can be with you, then I need —"

You…

"Yeah, *me.*"

Why you?

"Why me?"

Why, oh, why, why, why?

"You have the nerve to ask *me* why? You son of a   "

Be one bee, see one sea…

"What in the *fuck* are you —"

Why you? Why? Oh, why, why, why?

Having learned how to more lucidly control his dreams during his time alone in the Room, Keith has had enough of this shit and walks out, slamming the door behind him.

Much as he tries, though, Keith can never really escape the Room. Not as long as he sleeps, anyway, so he spends the weekend trying to stay awake. Gets outside in the crisp air, walks and sits on park benches until dusk, drinks coffee in diners until dawn. Avoids going home to The Wellraven, but he's starting to attract suspicious looks for his loitering, and he keeps encountering strange people on the streets who won't stop trying to shove flyers in his hand or repeating numbers and asking him, "Why, oh, why, why?" and he's just tired, so tired…so sick of it all.

And so today finds Keith on the couch again, enough left in his bagged bottle for another happy hour or two, three, four…

He's partially propped up against the back cushion with a flared pant leg folded under him, and, tucked under his floral-striped shirt where it's unbuttoned over his chest, a hand rests on his pec and scratches his armpit occasionally.

He didn't go to the park today. Hasn't gone anywhere. Just slept in and kept the shades drawn and watched the actor who ended up landing his role in daytime drama. Saw Lucinda, too, in yet another of her speaking parts. All day, he lounges here, soap after soap, game show after game show, never seeing himself brush his teeth or chew gum in ads anymore, and if he did, he'd hardly recognize himself.

Instead, he watches livelier, juicier guys take the lead as he just takes a swig, adjusts the crotch of his corduroys, and eases even farther down on the cushions, crushing the colonial barnyard under his ass. Sleep can come find him — the woman in the walls, too, so he can finally get fucked. Keith doesn't care anymore, doesn't think he'll have to cope with it for much longer. He just needs to build up the nerve…or deaden it enough.

A creaking in the dining room again. Huffing, Keith drags himself up to trudge around his bamboo-and-glass coffee table and turn the volume dial up on the television.

Creak.

Squeak.

That fucking lamp. That fucking couple upstairs — literally. Fucking. They've gone at it like rabbits since summer and don't seem to care the neighbors can hear. Hats off to Amy, but if she only knew how it could torture Keith sometimes.

The apartment's lit enough by the television for Keith to see the wicker lamp actually looks still this time. Not swinging on its chain and causing the creak. Fine, then it's a bedframe or something upstairs or next door. But just as Keith looks beyond the dining furniture to the wall, fearing the necklace could be back, the telephone starts ringing.

Again.

The trilling bell resonates through his bones, and he's frozen for the moment, the breath caught in his chest and his entire skeleton held captive by tightened muscles and tendons, unrelenting in their grip. As happened earlier, his ears are muffled to any other sound, nothing coming from the television or traffic or the elevator out in the hall, just this incessant ringing that finally compels him to furiously lurch for the phone and rip it from the wall.

Except Keith almost falls backward from a lack of resistance, skipping a few steps back and nearly tripping over the bamboo table behind his calves, the phone cradled in his arms and cord dangling in his hand. It was already detached from the wall, from when he'd disconnected it weeks ago…

He remembers that now, pulling the plug before the calls even had a chance to dry up on their own — before he'd have to admit to anyone else what a failure he is. How he's nothing without Rod and can't do this on his own. Can't keep pretending to be someone else for a living when his life is all an act offscreen, too.

Staring at the four-pronged jack hanging like dead weight from his grasp, Keith just stands there, blinking back tears as the telephone keeps ringing against his chest, where's he clutching it. Trembling, he drops the cord from his right hand and unsteadily lifts the receiver, bringing it to his ear.

"H-hello?"

The sizzle of static, faint then growing louder until it's almost like bacon frying in his ear canal. Keith holds the handset away, fearful of electricity zapping him. But, sensing the crackle quieting down again, he brings the earpiece closer and, this time, hears a couple of pulses tick through as if he were dialing. Another one just for a beat, then two more, and then a string of several pulses repeated over and over before returning to static. And then, once again:

Tick-tick.

Tick.

Tick-tick.

Tick-tick-tick-tick-tick-tick-tick-tick-tick.

Tick-tick-tick-tick-tick-tick-tick-tick.

Tick-tick-tick-tick-tick-tick-tick-tick-tick.

Tick-tick-tick-tick-tick-tick-tick-tick-tick-tick.

Tick-tick-tick-tick-tick-tick-tick-tick-tick.

Tick-tick-tick-tick-tick-tick-tick-tick-tick.

Tick-tick-tick-tick-tick-tick-tick-tick-tick.

And then it's back to one or two pulses before the longer strings repeat once more.

Keith replaces the receiver and lets the entire phone fall to the carpet with a plasticky clack and an indignant *ding* from the ringer inside.

He can hear the sound of his own breathing again, along with a jaunty jig that plays behind him from a Lucky Charms ad.

Lucky charm…

Numb, he steps over the phone and walks to the dining room wall, where it could simply be a shiny glint of glue now winking at him from the tear in the paper, but he doesn't think so.

Peeling the strip that's now widened to two inches and is several in length, he's no longer stunned when the gold necklace drops to the floor. He stoops to grasp it, and it almost burns against his skin as he stands up straight again, but he isn't sure if it's hot or cold — and either way, it's not uncomfortable, feels natural somehow, igniting something in his veins. Somehow, he knows what he has to do, what he should have done long ago, but he's still afraid. Rubbing his thumb across the coin pendant, he next brings it to his lips and closes his eyes on a firm inhale.

He feels so stupid for even thinking it, but at this point anything goes.

So, running with his whiskey-logged logic, Keith takes a cue from the Bradys and wonders if, just like Bobby returned the tiki idol to its cave, perhaps bringing this necklace to the bedroom he's sealed off might break his curse, too. He hasn't set foot in there since it was confirmed that Rod had shacked up with Ty in Toronto, another promising young thing for him to lap up and spew out in time. Until then, the necklace had sat in there on the little round table next to Rod's usual side of the bed, all boxed up and wrapped in a bow as Keith's thank-you for securing him what was sure to be a successful audition. A gig that would've paved the way in more gold, figuratively, as Keith gained greater security in his finances and in himself, able to provide more to the life he wanted with Rod, a secret life lived in comfort with each other better than no life together at all, right?

Rounding the bend past the kitchen counter toward his unit door, he stops outside the master bedroom. Presses a palm against the plywood door before easing his hand down to the knob. The brass twists easily in his grip, and though he lets go in a moment of hesitation, the door slowly creaks open on its own.

Muscle memory leads him down a short faux-wood-paneled hall — the en-suite bathroom to his left and walk-in closet to his right — and straight back to the window, where he yanks the pull chain of a hanging lamp in the corner. The light corralled by a marigold velvet cylinder shade beams down on a small bamboo bistro table beside the balcony door. The amber glass ashtray resting on the rattan tabletop still holds the cremated remains of Rod's Camels, which Keith only let him smoke in this room or, preferably, out on the balcony. He hated the habit himself and hoped his lover would kick it, too — though not even Keith could begrudge him a post-coital smoke in reward for his own relaxed state, too boneless and melted in the golden sheets to care. Actually, he enjoyed breathing in the vapors Rod would blow into his mouth, his tongue following soon after for a repeat performance. The wind always did billow back into his sails before too long, among Rod's many other natural talents.

The bedsheets are still tangled from when Keith last kicked around in them, alone and far from satisfied that time. He sits at the edge of the bed now to run his hands over the silken fabric, unwashed since Rod last sweat into them, too. Keith kisses the pendant in his palm and lays it in the divot on Rod's pillow. Then, easing himself up and onto the other side of the bed, he rests his head on his own pillow, lying on his back and frowning at the popcorn ceiling.

He breathes in deeply, both proud and regretful of taking this step. The musk of woody cologne and tobacco and a sweet tang that was all Rod's own melds into a dangerous alchemy, opening portals in Keith's mind and stabbing his heart. Instantly, it's like no time has passed, and he can expect Rod to waltz inside this room after a long day at work has left him tipsy and drowsy yet spicy and horny and open to anything Keith wants to do to him. And sometimes, all they wanted to do was lie entwined as they listened to records and talked. Or didn't talk, just ran fingers through each other's hair, finding expression through the music, that shared experience of vibration on vinyl.

Propping his head on his hand, Keith glances over at the record player on his dresser, near the foot of the bed. Eyes the albums lined up vertically on the floor, leaning precariously against the dresser's edge. After a moment gliding his gaze along their well-worn edges, an album on the end tips over.

He sits up and crawls the length of the bed, then onto the floor to investigate. Fleetwood Mac's *Bare Trees* has fallen over to reveal very lush trees instead—the thick trunk of one grows in the foreground, with a couple lying beneath it, basking. Serene. One with nature. Just being…

Be one. Be.

Be one bee.

The voice from the Room resurfaces in Keith's memory, but he doesn't want to hear this nonsensical message again. Reaching for the record, he slips the vinyl from the sleeve and loads it on the turntable, resting the needle in place to hear John Lennon sing to himself and Yoko that everything would be all right, that when you're alone you just have to remember to "Hold On."

Sinking back to the floor to the mellow tune, Keith slumps against the mattress, all too aware that he has no one else but himself. But he doesn't know how much longer he can hold on…

Just when the gentle, encouraging melody has lulled him into at least a false sense of peace, the beat picks up as the next song struts in with an unsettling reminder of "freaks" on the telephone that won't leave him alone—the phone. Who was on its other end? Who was dialing from his? How was it ringing in the first place?

Curling his knees up to his chin, Keith dips his head and presses his eyes into them. He clutches at his unruly hair, understanding fully now how much he's lost his grip, not just in these bizarre past days but long before that...

Lennon sings of parents who didn't want him so made him a star, and Keith cringes at how he himself only sought fame so he could make his mom and dad proud, believe that he was "somebody," anybody other than who he really is. That's why acting was a natural choice. Only when the curtain dropped behind him and he could be in this room alone with Rod could Keith drop the script, too, and let his lover wipe away the makeup, peel away his costume, keeping the door ajar but never fully open. "I Found Out," Lennon belts out, and finding out has always been Keith's fear.

He scrambles to his feet and lifts the needle to drop it somewhere else, but when the melancholy notes of "Isolation" start hammering on his heartstrings instead, he snatches the record up and flips it over, as if hiding the printed titles of Side A will erase the words already out in the air and replaying in Keith's thoughts. Clipping the tonearm in its rest instead of playing anything more, he flops back down on the bed, this time on his stomach so he can cry into his pillow.

"Rod," he sobs into the cushion, then he reaches for the one beside him and hugs it close, so close it brings the coin back to his lips, and he speaks against it as he continues to cry. "I get it. I get it. I know you don't want me. I can't have you the way I want you, but I need you. Can't you come back just to help me find my way? Help me be more like you?" Sniffing against the dampened pillowcase, he shakes his head. "Be more like...me?"

Be one.

Be.

Why you?

Why, oh, why, why, why?

"I don't understand..." he whimpers and, in exhaustion, slips to sleep.

We never use this room. Why don't we ever use this room?

"No need," Keith says, looking around the master bedroom this time, which is covered in gold silk sheets.

But this room is nice. Like, really nice. And look at the size of it! Bigger than the one you've been using.

"It's no use, Rod. Not without you here."

But, Keith…I am here. I've been right here, this entire time.

Keith squints at the rectangular furnishing nearest him and pulls off its shiny cover to reveal his turntable on the dresser.

Stereo, too, Rod says. *Not a fine one, not top-of-the-line one, but a good one. Why won't you use this?*

"Because it reminds me too much of you."

Don't you want to remember?

"Remember…?" Only then does it occur to Keith that, when he finally raises his gaze, he's able to look right at his companion — not a shadow, not a vague, glitching figure but Roderick. Not in the flesh, but as clear as. He's smiling at Keith from within a soft, ethereal glow, but it's him, from the twinkle and crinkle of his eye as he flashes that lopsided grin to the little dark hairs that pepper his large tanned hands. Keith wants nothing more than to launch himself over the bed and into Rod's arms, to kiss him senselessly and beg him never to leave again, but there's a sadness in that smile that tells him, more permanently than anything ever could, that as sure as he's here now, he really and truly cannot stay.

Wild, man…right? Rod huffs out a light yet forced laugh, arms spread out as he looks himself up and down.

"Too late," Keith says, feeling he's heard these words before, this whole conversation, more or less. His posture sinks as the life force seems to drain from him and gravity pulls him down, down.

It is *too late, isn't it*, he says without speech, swallowing the hardening knot in his throat as Rod communicates to him without words, too — volumes, in what seems like seconds. Keith can't bear it, can't even squeak out, *Oh, Roderick.*

His smile cracking as his cheeks twitch and his eyes well, Rod drops his hands and shrugs, scans the space surrounding him as if he isn't even sure where he is.

It's cool in here, he says as he looks around, continuing to echo Keith's words from the original dream. *I'm actually cold.*

But then he looks back at Keith meaningfully, growing fainter within the ever-brightening room.

But it's not too late. Is it? For you?

"Remember..."

Musk and smoke fill his nostrils, and Keith wakes to music.

"Remember...remember...remember..."

The needle is skipping on the vinyl that's started spinning again, the tonearm off its rest.

"Remember...remember...remember..."

Squeezing his eyes closed, Keith then opens them to the cold metal still pressed to his face. Lifting it from the fabric as he rolls over onto his side, dangling in front of him isn't the gold coin pendant but Rod's dog tags, hanging from their silver chain.

"What would you like me to remember, Rod?" he whispers, his voice dragged across gravel.

After skipping on the word *sorry* a few times, the tonearm lifts the needle and sets it down on "Love," letting the whole song play through.

The silver chain is intact, and Keith slips it around his neck. Slides a tag between his lips and bites down.

Nuzzling into the pillows and underneath the bedsheet, he feels a light, recurring pressure on his hair, and he closes his eyes to the caress. Allows the sweet, haunting melody to soothe and bathe him in the truth. What he and Rod shared…it wasn't all in his head. Was everything in his heart. His gut.

Yet even though he knows this now, has always known, it's just as real as the knowing that they'd never last. Because Rod didn't last. The same heart that would've led him back from Canada—to Keith—took him out of this world first.

Keith's face breaks beneath the weight of this knowledge, and he draws the sheet over his head. He feels less alone now as his lover serenades him from the ether, yet he still doesn't know how to navigate any of this on his own.

Delicate notes on the piano fade out, and guitar strums in the next song waste no time making their presence known. The bass beat jolts Keith from the quiet cocoon he's tried to wrap himself in, lose himself in, distracted from scheming how to join Rod where he is…forever.

He knows Rod wouldn't want that. But it's not up to him, now is it? He might've saved Keith before, but he'd probably sapped his energy in the effort, and that's why it took him a while to come back. Visiting in dreams is one thing, but these physical feats around the apartment have got to be tapping him out again. Rod can't keep it up for long.

Before Keith can contemplate any further how he might try pills, maybe even the roof next time, the record skips, and he hears "Look at Me." As gentle as "Love," it's like Rod is telling Keith, insisting to him, that he's here and asking what he should do.

"You don't have to do anything, my love," Keith says. "You can help me by doing nothing this time."

But the record skips and replays the bridge over and over again, like Rod's begging Keith to look at him, reminding him again that he's here.

"Ohhh, my love."

Keith shakes his head, only for the needle to skip to another song, playing just the word *why.*

"You know why, Rod."

"...you..."

The tonearm had to skip back to "Look at Me" for that one. This is going to drain Rod fast, and then he really won't be able to stand in Keith's way.

Why again. Then an *oh* and back to *why*, which now just keeps repeating.

Why you, why, oh, why, why, why?

"Why me? Why *you*, Rod? Why does it make any more sense for *you* to be dead? Why *not* me?" For as angry and determined as he's growing, Keith only cries harder and falters in resolve.

But again, the tonearm repositions itself and skips out the same refrain:

Why you, why, oh, why, why, why?

Keith can't take it anymore. Whipping the sheet off himself, he leaps to his feet and rips the record off the turntable, flinging it to the carpet like a frisbee.

"Enough," he cries. "Just be at peace and let me find mine. Let me find it with you."

But no sooner has he gained the upper hand when he hears that damned telephone ringing again. Ringing, ringing, endlessly ringing, shrill and desperate.

Keith flies out of the bedroom on the remaining fumes of his whiskey, sure he's left a gouge in the paneling by shoving the already-open door against it so hard on his way out. The phone keeps ringing from where it lies on the matted shag carpet, the handset not even in its cradle but lying faceup. Keith kneels down to it and screams into the mouthpiece, *"WHAT?"*

The crackle of static again, but when it goes quiet, he presses the earpiece to his head. The same pulsing as before:

Tick-tick.

Tick.

Tick-tick.

Tick-tick-tick-tick-tick-tick-tick-tick-tick.

Tick-tick-tick-tick-tick-tick-tick-tick.

Tick-tick-tick-tick-tick-tick-tick-tick-tick.

Tick-tick-tick-tick-tick-tick-tick-tick-tick-tick.

Tick-tick-tick-tick-tick-tick-tick-tick-tick.

Tick-tick-tick-tick-tick-tick-tick-tick-tick.

Tick-tick-tick-tick-tick-tick-tick-tick-tick.

"What the fuck is this supposed to mean? Are you dialing an actual fucking number?"

On that last thought, Keith manages to calm down for a second, taking a moment to breathe deeply in and out as his own words register to him. The pulsing: it's the same sound he'd hear in the receiver if he were dialing, the number of pulses equaling the digit dialed—except for zero, which would pulse ten times.

As the pulsing continues in his ear, he picks the base of the phone up in his other hand and rises to his feet, walking to the counter to rest it where it usually sits and glancing around the rest of the kitchen and dining area frantically for a pen. Holding the handset to his ear with his shoulder, he stretches the curled cord around and over the counter as he enters the kitchen and finds a pencil in a drawer, but he can't find any paper. Winding back to the dining room, he rips the torn wallpaper strip from the wall with surprising satisfaction and holds it down on the Formica tabletop as he counts out the pulses and records them on paper.

Tick-tick—two.

Tick—one.

Tick-tick—two.

And so on until he's written, *2129890999*.

Repeating it back to himself out loud, he has a flash of memory back to the strangers who approached him on the street over the weekend, seemingly senile or intoxicated and reciting what he thought were random numbers. A lot of nines, he remembers, just like this, and they'd also ask him—

Turning from the table toward the counter, he steps up to the phone to inspect its rotary dial and the letters printed around it with each number.

The number one stands alone, but two is paired with *ABC*. So the local 2 1 2 area code could be considered *A-1-A* or another letter combination, like *A 1 B* or *B 1 C* or…

B-1-B.

C-1-C.

Be one bee.

See one sea.

Keith's stomach tightens like a fist around the thoughts he has next. On another deep breath, he grabs the phone's wall cord and lures in the jack. Plugging it back into the wall, he can hear the normal ringtone. From inside New York City, he wouldn't need to dial the area code, but that was a nice touch on Rod's part. Always so thorough, so precise, and the smaller numbers had a better chance of being recognized. As for the rest…

Keith's hand and head are sweating against the receiver, though a coolness washes over him, too, and the skin of his forearms and shins prickles. His chest expands as he inserts a numbed fingertip, its nail chewed to the quick, into a hole in the circular plastic and dials *Y* (nine), then *U* (eight).

Why you.

As the dial slowly spins its way back counterclockwise, a trembling finger waits for the second-to-last hole to reach *WXY* again. Nine. *Y.* When it does, Keith drags it back around to the metal finger stop on the other side. Then he dials zero, which he got from the ten pulses he'd counted earlier. And though it's associated with the operator and not the letter *O*, he usually pronounces *0* the same way. A lot of people do. Rod no exception.

Why, oh.

Finally, Keith dials and waits out the nine-pulse ticking of each *Y, Y, Y* with a patience he's never known.

Why, why, why.

He knows the call has connected when he can hear a tone signaling that the phone's ringing on the other end. The grip on his stomach has traveled all the way up to his throat, and he rakes his free hand through his hair before bringing it back around to bite his fingernail, holding his breath.

After another rapid heartbeat or two, there's a click as someone picks up.

"Hello, Gay Switchboard of New York," a kind voice answers.

Keith strangles the handset in his clammy palm, lowering it to his heart as both his face and chest scrunch into a still, silent sob. His eyelids feel like they can barely contain his eyes, which are bursting from their sockets as his lungs deflate, and his sternum seems ready to crack. Clenching in on himself like this, he heaves against the phone pressed to his chest with a stifled mewl.

Oh my God, Roderick. I love you.

"Hello?"

He hears the muffled voice against his chest hair as he shakily draws a measured breath in through his nose and funnels the exhale through O-shaped lips, trying to steady his fluttering diaphragm.

"Hello? Can I help you?" the smothered yet hopeful voice repeats.

Wincing, Keith jerks both head and shoulders in a collective nod. He presses his lips together and sniffs, then wipes some residual tears away from his squeezed-shut eyes.

I love you. I don't think I even realized how much until now. Thank you for loving me enough, too, to do this.

"Can I help who's there?"

Scraping the telephone handset up his chest and along his neck and cheek to his ear, Keith croaks out a syllable, then clears his throat before trying again.

"Yes, yeah. Hi," he says, running a quavering hand back through his wayward mane of hair and clutching a handful of it at the roots. "I…could really use someone to talk to."

THE END

Founded independently as the Gay Switchboard of New York in 1972, the LGBT Switchboard of New York is now administered by the LGBT National Help Center as the oldest LGBTQIA+ hotline in the world, offering free and confidential support. They can be contacted at help@LGBThotline.org as well as the original phone number, which remains (212) 989-0999 to this day.

Acknowledgments

My sincerest thanks to all the authors who contributed to the original *Ghosts & Gravity* anthology's success, especially those who directly collaborated with me to develop crossovers between our stories: D.L. Hartman ("BellaLoki"), Morgan and Jennifer Locklear ("Robert"), Shani Struthers ("The Guardian"), Susan Swords ("Harry Nilsson Was Right"), Ai Tran ("The Man in White"), and Becca Vry ("Chrysalide").

Much gratitude to Locklear Books for inviting me into this ghostly and grave world in the first place! Your clever concept was something I truly couldn't turn down and an inspiration to write again after a long hiatus. I adored haunting the halls of The Wellraven. And I could cry over Michael Wolfe's moving voice work in "Ghosted" for the anthology's audiobook — my first title ever told through this medium. Many thanks as well to Jocqueline Protho of The Audio Flow, LLC, for her award-winning direction and cameo in the audio version of my story.

I can't lie, though…having to set this story in 1972 (per the anthology's parameters) was a challenge for me. Typically, I prefer my stuffy Victorians and spiffy Flappers. So thank you, *The Brady Bunch*, for finally getting me excited about polyester and macramé. "Fright Night" is my favorite episode of that show ('cause you know I love a ghostie, even the fake ones), so it was absolute fate that it first broadcast in 1972, as did the Bradys' Hawaiian holiday (which is another favorite because…tiki! Who knew that program was so paranormal?!). John Lennon's *Plastic Ono Band* album deserves thanks, too, for helping me develop Keith's pivotal scene with the record player and for giving Roderick a voice. And as long as I'm thanking TV shows and vinyl records, why not give a tarot deck a high five, too, as the *Morgan-Greer Tarot* genuinely helped me brainstorm my central characters and conflicts, showing me a deeper and truer love there than I had originally envisioned. And let's face it: its marvelous mustaches and psychedelic style got me into the groooovy groove of this seventies story.

But back to *people*…Authors Nicki Elson and Shani Struthers, you are my tried and trues. Heartfelt thanks for your beta-reading and feedback. And, as always, so much gratitude to Coreen Montagna and Gina Dickerson, whose interior and exterior designs make the literary so lovely.

Limitless thanks, too, of course, to the family and friends who've always cheered on what I accomplish and what I have the potential to. Though my dad didn't live to see this story published, he was alive when I wrote it and has infused his confidence in me into it as well.

Not everyone, however, gets to enjoy their basic right to be loved for who they are. For the organizations that offer safe space and support—like the LGBT Switchboard of New York and LGBT National Help Center—this world owes a debt of gratitude.

About the Author

Rumer Haven is probably the most social recluse you could ever meet. When she's not babbling her fool head off among friends and family, she's pacified with a good story that she's reading, writing, or revising—or binge-watching *Buffy*. A writer/editor hailing from Chicago, she presently lives in London with her husband and probably a ghost or two. Rumer has always had a penchant for the past and paranormal, which inspires her writing to explore dimensions of time, love, and the soul. Her award-winning work includes *Coattails and Cocktails* (First Prize Winner, 2018 *Red City Review* Book Awards) and *What the Clocks Know* (First Place Winner in General Fiction, 2017 *Red City Review* Book Awards).

Visit Rumer at:
www.rumerhaven.com
@RumerHaven

Myths, Mothers, and Mystics

A Short Story Collection

A goddess brings a statue to life
so it can become the sculptor's wife.

A mirror reflects more than what should appear
as a bride's big day is filled with fear.

New tech revolutionizes reproductive rights
while ghost hunters fill an innkeeper's night with frights.

And just when she falls out of love's blinding spell,
a tattoo artist checks into a haunted hotel.

In this speculative fiction collection, feminism meets folklore, fantasy, and science fiction as Rumer Haven shares some of the more random yarns she's spun over the past decade and a half. From ancient Cyprus to modern Sedona, *Myths, Mothers, and Mystics* tells the tales of women who must find — if not fight — their way against the natural and supernatural.

Coattails and Cocktails

A body clearly shaken, but not stirring…

Summer, 1929. Murder isn't on the menu when Chicago tycoon Ransom Warne hosts a dinner party at his country estate. But someone's a victim—and everyone's a suspect—when drinks and desires lead to disaster.

Hollywood starlet Lottie Landry has returned home to celebrate her engagement. She's famous for her on- and off-screen romance with co-star Noble, but, privately, she's having second thoughts. As her former guardian, Ransom doesn't approve of the match. Yet his own affections raise questions when his wife, Edith, suspects him of having an affair—just as Noble suspects Lottie. Stirred into the mix are Lottie's friends Helen and Rex, a young journalist and football hero who can feel tension building in the Warne mansion like a shaken champagne bottle.

And once the cork pops, a body drops.

Coattails and Cocktails is where Agatha Christie meets *The Great Gatsby*, a whodunit spiked with new love and old baggage, public faces and private vices. Filled to the brim with romance and mystery, it's sure to intoxicate. (First Prize Winner in the 2018 *Red City Review* Book Awards).

What the Clocks Know

Suffering a quarter-life crisis, twenty-six-year-old Margot sets out on a journey of self-discovery — she dumps her Boston boyfriend, quits her Chicago job, and crosses the ocean to crash at her friend's London flat.

Rather than find herself, though, she only feels more lost. An unsettling energy affects her from the moment she enters the old Victorian residence, and she spirals into depression. Frightened and questioning her perceptions, she gradually suspects her dark emotions belong to Charlotte instead.

Who is Charlotte? The name on a local gravestone could relate to Margot's dreams and the gray woman weeping at the window.

Finding a ghost isn't what she had in mind when she went "soul searching," but somehow Margot's future may depend on Charlotte's past.

Woven between the nineteenth and twenty-first centuries, *What the Clocks Know* is a haunting story of love and identity that won First Place in General Fiction in the 2017 *Red City Review* Book Awards.

Seven for a Secret

It's the year 2000, and twenty-four-year-old Kate moves into a new apartment to find a new state of independence in a new millennium. Almost immediately, she starts crushing on a hot guy who lives in her building. Deciding to take a break from her boyfriend Dexter, Kate believes the only thing now separating her from the fresh object of her sexual fantasies is the thin wall between their neighboring apartments.

A former 1920s hotel, Camden Court has housed many lonely lives over the decades — and is where a number of them have come to die. They're not all resting in peace, however, including ninety-year-old Olive, who dropped dead in Kate's apartment and continues to make her presence known.

For Olive has a secret she's dying to tell. One linking her to the sex, scandal, and sacrifice of a young dreamer named Lon. As the past haunts the present, Kate's romantic notion that the thrill-of-the-chase beats the reality-after-the-catch unexpectedly entwines her modern-day love life with Lon's Jazz Age tragedy.

With a little supernatural and a lotta' razzle-dazzle, *Seven for a Secret* is where historical fiction meets contemporary rom-com — from the Roaring Twenties when the "New Woman" was born, to the modern Noughties when she really came of age.